Brai

written by Jack Gabolinscy
illustrated by Robin Van't Hof

Theo's brain cells fizzed, popped and crackled like a billion bangers in a New Year's Eve fireworks display. He was having a brainstorm. As the bright ideas exploded through his head, he rushed about the house gathering the various items he needed to build a brilliant new Fish-Catching Contraption. He stacked the parts on the desk by his bed.

SUPE
GREATEST INVENTIONS

His computer would be the brains of the new invention, with a GPS system as the fish-finder. The eyes would be a web-cam and a powerful flashlight inside a diving helmet connected to a large television screen. His father's exercycle and a pair of giant flippers would provide power.

GPS
US DIVERS
DEEP PRESSURE

He chose the bath tub from the bathroom for the trap, and the bathmat rolled onto a curtain rod to be the trapdoor. His mother would be a little upset at first, but she would change her mind once she started getting fresh, fat fish for dinner. Lastly he discovered an old, meaty dog bone that had been buried in the garden for a couple of weeks. Its rotten smell was perfect for baiting a fish-trap.

Theo's brainstorm continued for two hours until he had completed his new invention. It looked more like the twisted wreckage left by a force ten tornado than a work of genius. A tangle of electric wires, ropes, sticky tapes, hoses, mirrors, screens and other gear filled his room and disappeared down the passage into the bathroom. It looked like an enormous tarantula's web!

GPS

"Cool!" exclaimed Theo with satisfaction. "Time for a trial run." He booted up the computer, entered ***Destination Back Yard Pond*** and clicked ***Go.***

The Fish-Catching Contraption issued a series of sparks and high-pitched squeals. The exercycle spun, the flippers flapped, the web-cam and flashlight beam shone and rotated inside the diver's helmet. Lights and humming noises throbbed through the tangle of wires. The bathtub clanked and rocked.

The TV screen flashed like a rainbow; it zoomed like a powerful telescope checking on a far planet. Then, quite suddenly, everything became peaceful. The screen picture focused itself perfectly. The Fish-Catching Contraption was successfully settled in the back yard pond!

GREATEST INVENTION
HOW THINGS WORK
REMOTE OPERATED GUIDE
A-Z ALIEN LIFEFORMS
OUTER SPACE
FROM MARS

Theo rushed to the bathroom. He unrolled the bathmat. The bath was full of water weeds, pond water, and fifteen goldfish. "Cool – I'm a genius!" he boasted. Back at the computer, he entered the instruction, ***Return to pond.*** With a splash, a gurgle and a chug from the exercycle, the goldfish and most of the weeds and water disappeared from the bathroom.

1st
1st SCIENCE AWARD

Theo's eyes shone with excitement as he typed ***Destination Pacific Ocean*** into his computer and pressed ***Go.*** The trap shuddered, the exercycle spun, the web-cam turned, the wires hummed and the bathtub rocked. The TV screen focused and refocused, then suddenly became clear and still. The Fish-Catching Contraption was safely moved to somewhere in the middle of the Pacific Ocean!

GREATEST INVENTION
HOW THINGS WORK
REMOTE OPERATED GUIDE
A-Z ALIEN LIFEFORMS
OUTER SPACE
FISHING SPOTS

The underwater world was wonderful. There were coral reefs, forests of swaying seaweed, crayfish, giant clams, beautiful tropical fish, long slender eels, an octopus, a giant turtle and schools of fish of every kind. “Cool,” chuckled Theo. “Now where’s dinner?”

As he asked, a huge snapper swam into the bath. Perfect! ***Close the trap*** he entered. But he was a moment too slow. Unseen by him, just off screen, an enormous mako shark had been stalking the snapper. At the same time as Theo hit ***Enter,*** the shark flicked its tail and attacked.

There was a flash of red and black. The trapdoor zapped closed, and with a mighty clank the Fish-Catching Contraption landed back in the bathroom.

Theo rushed to look, but again he was too slow. His mother was there first.

“What’s this?” she shrieked, waving at the disgusting mess of frothy water, sand and seaweed sloshed about the bathroom. “Whatever have you been up to now, Theo?”

Theo knew his mother's mood would improve once she saw the wonderful snapper he had caught for dinner, so he unrolled the bathmat. "Look, Mother," he smiled, "Snapper for dinner." But there was no snapper. Instead there was a very large, very angry mako shark showing its teeth and glaring up at them.

Theo entered ***"Return to the Pacific"*** onto the computer, and clicked ***"Go".*** The shark disappeared, but much of the seaweed, sand and a slithering moray eel remained. "Sorry, Mother. I seem to have made a messy mistake. I'll clean up after lunch."

"You will clean up **before** lunch, thank you," said his mother, but she was too late. The bathroom mess had instantly triggered Theo's over-active imagination. The fizz, pop and crackle of a new brainstorm was already exploding behind his eyes.